MW00814301

NOW
THAT I'M HERE
BY AARON MESHON
Dial Books for Young Readers

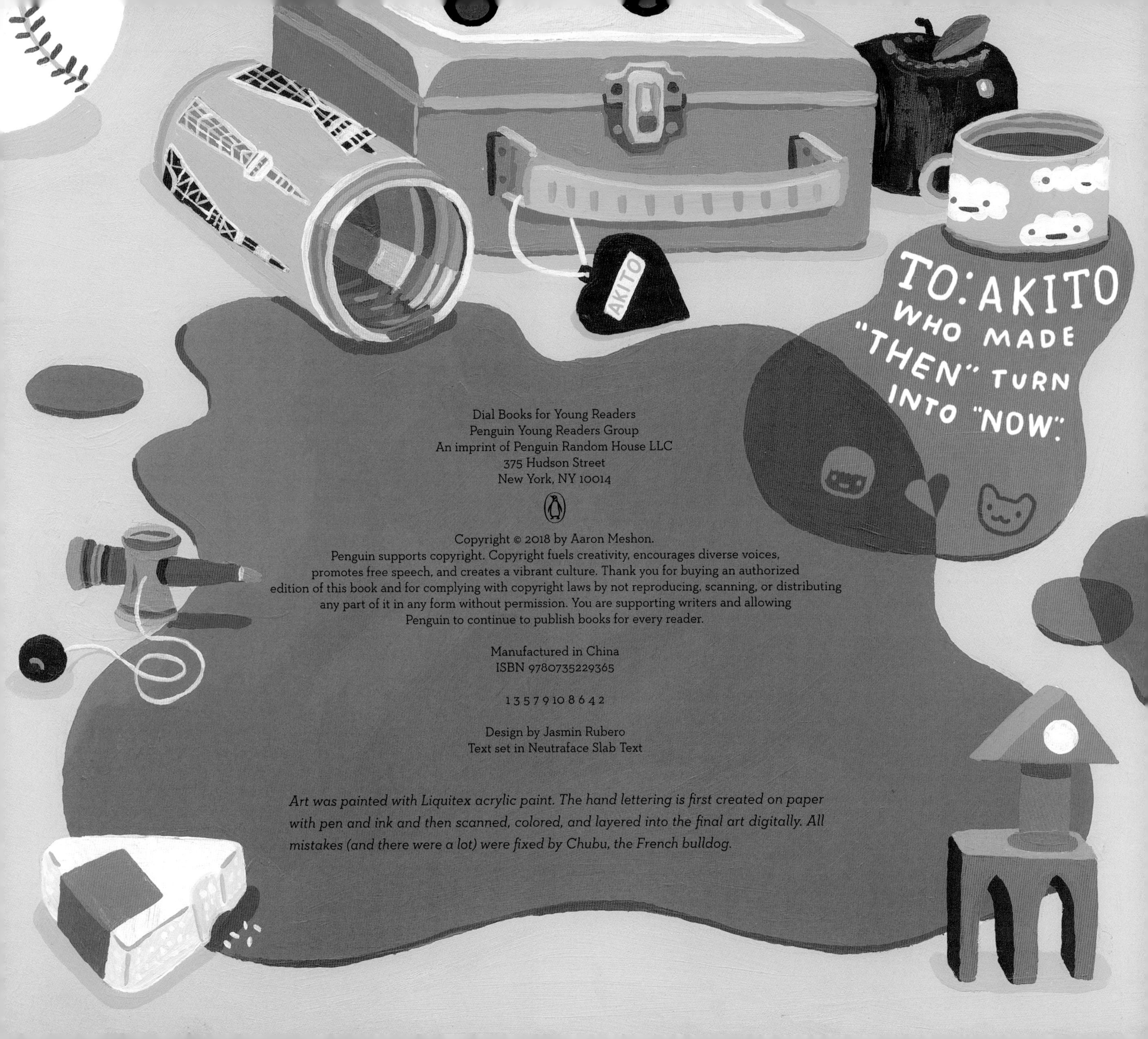

Dial Books for Young Readers
Penguin Young Readers Group
An imprint of Penguin Random House LLC
375 Hudson Street
New York, NY 10014

Copyright © 2018 by Aaron Meshon.
Penguin supports copyright. Copyright fuels creativity, encourages diverse voices, promotes free speech, and creates a vibrant culture. Thank you for buying an authorized edition of this book and for complying with copyright laws by not reproducing, scanning, or distributing any part of it in any form without permission. You are supporting writers and allowing Penguin to continue to publish books for every reader.

Manufactured in China
ISBN 9780735229365

1 3 5 7 9 10 8 6 4 2

Design by Jasmin Rubero
Text set in Neutraface Slab Text

Art was painted with Liquitex acrylic paint. The hand lettering is first created on paper with pen and ink and then scanned, colored, and layered into the final art digitally. All mistakes (and there were a lot) were fixed by Chubu, the French bulldog.

Before I arrived

Mom and Dad dreamed of me.

They couldn't wait

to meet me.
MEET WHO?

Before me, life was really boring.

Now that I'm here, life is so fun.

Breakfast used to be super dull.

Now breakfast is so awesome.

Mom and Dad had all of this useless stuff:

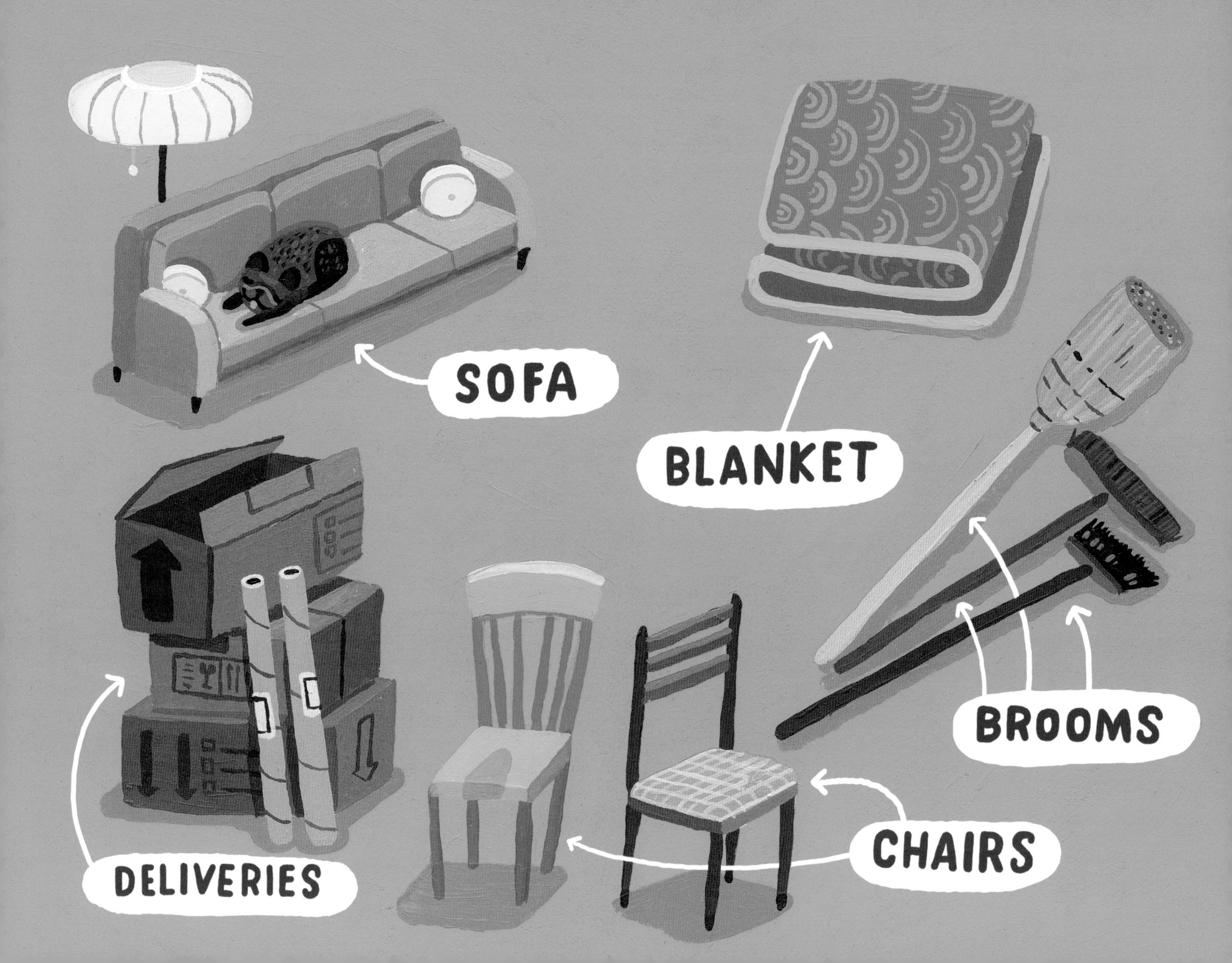

Now we have:

THE TERRIFIC TENT
A COOL CAVE
THE FANTASTIC FORT
A GREAT GATE

DEFEND

THAT WAS MY BED!

THE FORT!

TIME TO
GET
FOR WORK!
THEY ARE LATE AGAIN!

READY!
AND SCHOOL!

NOW WE HAVE FUN

RIDING THE TRAIN

Mom and Dad used to rush to work.

Now they take forever!

Everybody is

working hard now!

At lunchtime:

Dad used to get 

. Mom used to get 

.

Now lunch is way better!

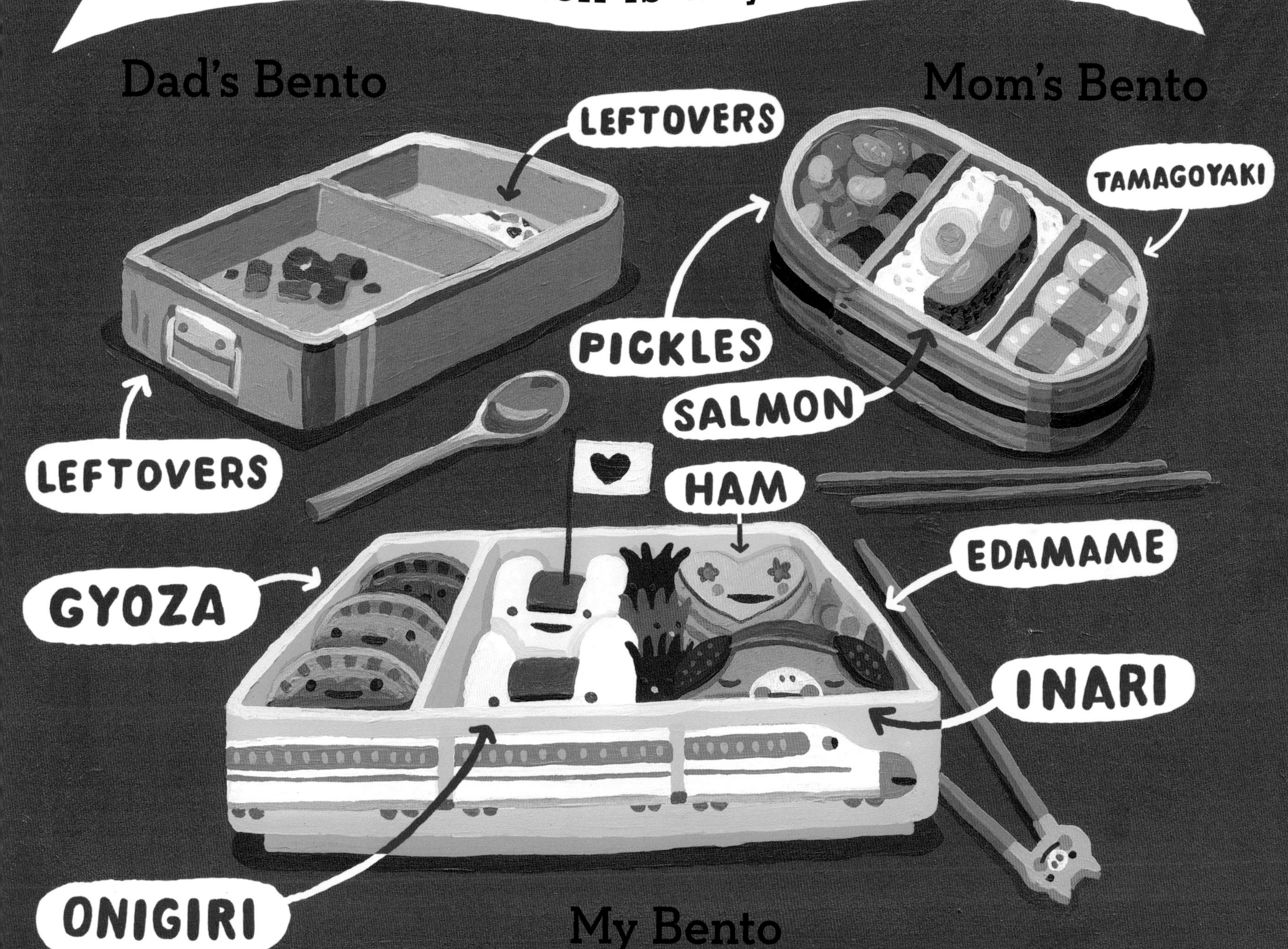

NAP

TIME!

After work Mom and Dad
used to rush home.

Now we take our time
through the park.

We explore all

the fun places.

Now Mom and Dad have

tons of new friends.

WE'RE HOME!

AND NOW MY
FLOOR IS A
MESS!

Mom and Dad’s dinner used to arrive in 30 minutes or less.

Now dinner takes longer with chefs in training!

Mom and Dad used to read before bed.

Now we all do!

Before I arrived
life was
pretty humdrum,

and now . . .

It’s pretty awesome!